For the wonderful
Mendy.
with love
from
Jue

My Busy Day

by Jill Davis

illustrated by Jill Kastner

viking

COZY, dreamy, sleepyhead. Don't make me get out of bed.

Sisters, brothers,
three, then four,
Waiting at the
bathroom door.

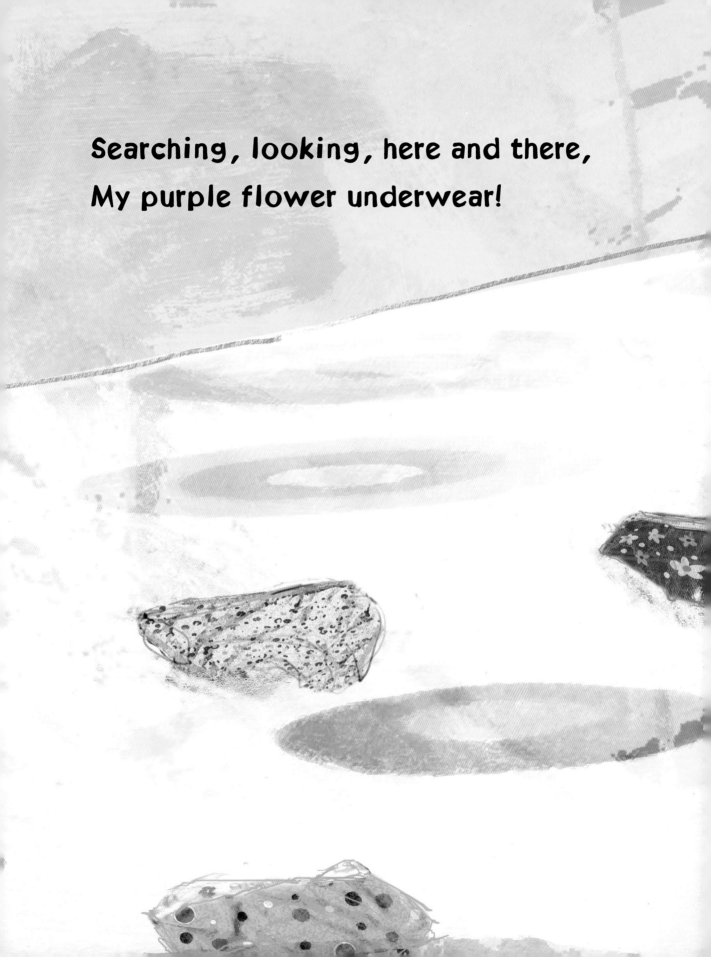

Searching, looking, here and there,
My purple flower underwear!

Finding one, but never two.
I'll never find my other shoe.

Yellow, yummy, warm, and runny,
Scrambled eggs look very funny.

Lunch box, juice box, mittens, hat,
A meow bye-bye from kitty cat.

Friends and toys and playing games.
At circle time we sing our names.

Lunchtime, fun time, fill my belly,
Peanut butter, smooth grape jelly.

A is for Apple

B is for Bumblebee.

Books and poems, reading time,

Pictures, stories,
words that rhyme.

Stretch out on a big rug map.

Rest your head and take a nap.

Day done, coat on, wait for Gram.

Here she comes with baby Sam!

Driving slowly, play a song.
I know how to sing along.

Dinner, bath time, rub-a-dub,

All the children, one big tub.

One more story?
Please, please, please?
Tuck us in so we
won't freeze.

Snug and warm.
Out goes the light.

Now we'll have
sweet dreams tonight.

Good night.

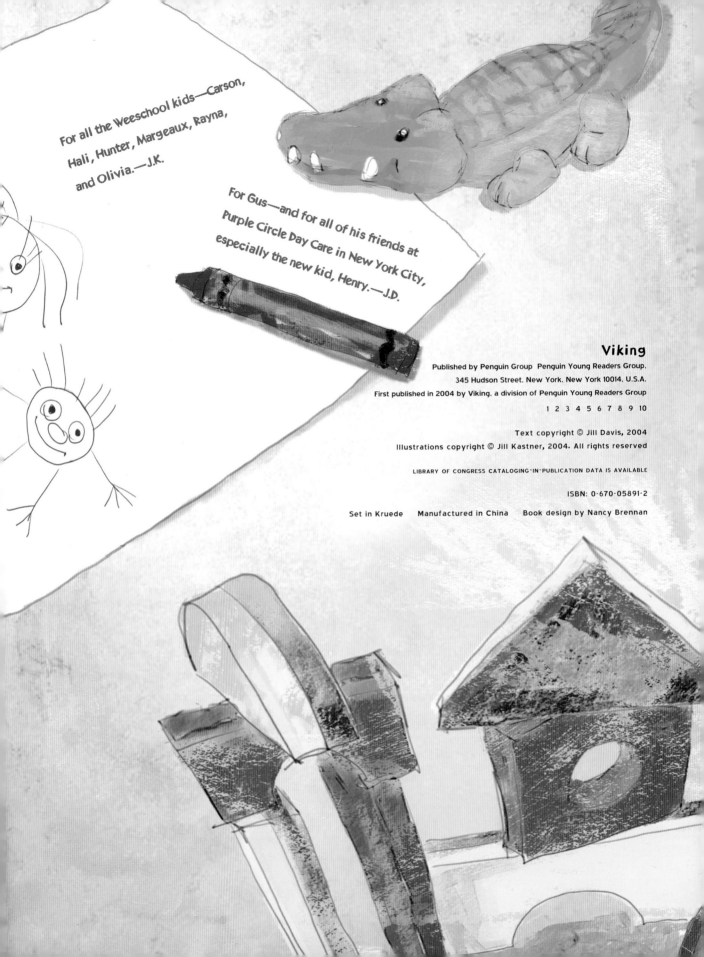

For all the Weeschool kids—Carson,
Hali, Hunter, Margeaux, Rayna,
and Olivia.—J.K.

For Gus—and for all of his friends at
Purple Circle Day Care in New York City,
especially the new kid, Henry.—J.D.

Viking

Published by Penguin Group Penguin Young Readers Group.
345 Hudson Street. New York. New York 10014. U.S.A.

First published in 2004 by Viking. a division of Penguin Young Readers Group

1 2 3 4 5 6 7 8 9 10

LIBRARY OF CONGRESS CATALOGING-IN-PUBLICATION DATA IS AVAILABLE

ISBN: 0-670-05891-2

Set in Kruede   Manufactured in China   Book design by Nancy Brennan